For Vivian – with love from us both

A Red Fox Book

Published by Random House Children's Books
20 Vauxhall Bridge Road, London SW1V 2SA

A division of Random House UK Ltd
London Melbourne Sydney Auckland
Johannesburg and agencies throughout the world

Copyright text © Diana Hendry 1995
Copyright illustrations © Sue Heap 1995

1 3 5 7 9 10 8 6 4 2

First published in Great Britain by Hutchinson Children's Books 1995

Red Fox edition 1999

Printed in Singapore

RANDOM HOUSE UK Limited Reg. No. 954009

ISBN 0 091 87297 9

HAPPY OLD BIRTHDAY, OWL

DIANA HENDRY

with illustrations by

SUE HEAP

RED FOX

It was early morning in the attic. When Raggy Christine woke up she saw that One-Eyed Penguin was crying. He was looking out of the window and as he cried his flippers quivered. At Christmas, Penguin had been given a new, second eye, but he hadn't yet learned to cry with both of them together.

Knitted Owl and Albapot were still asleep. Owl was snoring. Albapot's hat had fallen over her eyes.

"What's the matter?" asked Raggy Christine.

"Look," sniffed Penguin. "They're taking Our Child out without us!"

Raggy Christine looked and saw Mr Peppermint putting a picnic basket into the car and Mrs Peppermint carrying Lily in her best woolly bonnet.

Raggy Christine decided to join Penguin in a little sobbing. Owl snored on.

"What's all the fuss?" asked Albapot, appearing out of her hat.

"They're off on another jaunt without us," said Raggy Christine.

"And it was my turn to go with them," quivered Penguin.

Albapot climbed snappily up on to the window sill – she had new elastic bands in her legs – and looked out of the window.

"I suppose they'll come back," said Raggy Christine.

"Of course they'll come back," said Albapot crossly. "You know they *always* come back."

"Gone off without us," said a mournful voice. Owl had woken up. "And on my birthday."

Albapot, Raggy Christine and One-Eyed Penguin stared at him.

"Why didn't you tell us it was your birthday?" asked Albapot crossly.

There was a long silence.

"I've only just remembered," said Knitted Owl. "And a fine birthday it is when Your Child ups and offs without you."

"I've told you," snapped Albapot, "she'll be back. They'll all be back. Now let's cheer ourselves up and sing Happy Birthday to Owl. How old are you, Owl?"

Owl closed his eyes to think about this. "I was born..." began Owl. "I was born..." he tried again, "in 1905."

"That doesn't answer the question," said Albapot.

"It could be my fifteenth birthday," said Owl, "or it could be my fiftieth, or maybe my hundred and fiftieth, or..."

"All right. Don't go on anymore," said Albapot. "Can anyone here count beyond ten?"

Nobody could.

"We'll just have to say it's your Very Old Birthday," said Albapot.

" I think I'll go back to sleep," said Owl. "Being left behind and not knowing how old I am. It's all very tiring. Could you sing Happy Birthday later?"

"Of course we could," said Raggy Christine. "You go back to sleep, Owl, and when you wake up we can have a party. Exactly *when* do you think Our Child will come back, Albapot?"

"Later," said Albapot. "And don't keep asking."

Owl was very good at sleeping. He was snoring again within minutes.

"What are we going to do?" asked Penguin, all of a flap. "We need presents and party hats and a cake."

Albapot adjusted her own hat. "We'll have to go downstairs," she said.

"Downstairs!" gasped Raggy Christine and Penguin together, and for a moment the thought of the Great Downstairs made them forget all about Mr and Mrs Peppermint and Lily.

"Downstairs," said Albapot firmly and she marched snappily to the attic door and flung it open.

Raggy Christine gazed down the long staircase.

"I feel a bit dizzy," she said.

"Hold my flipper," said Penguin.

"If you took your hair out of your eyes it would help," said Albapot sliding briskly down the bannisters.

Penguin found it easier to go down the stairs backwards. Raggy Christine went down on her bottom.

"This is His and Her bedroom," announced Albapot.

"They've got a very big cot," said Penguin peering up at the bed.

But Raggy Christine had found the jewellery box on the dressing table and picked out a necklace of brightly coloured beads.

"Owl would love these," she said. "This will be *my* birthday present."

Up in the attic, Owl dreamed of Time passing...

HAPPY
1ST
BIRTHDAY

When Penguin saw the bathroom he got very excited.

"I could have a bath," he said. "I could flip and flap and flop."

"We haven't got time for flipping and flapping and flopping," said Albapot firmly. "It's Owl's Very Old Birthday we're thinking about. We need to go down to the kitchen."

"More stairs," said Raggy Christine. "I haven't the legs for stairs."

"Try the bannisters with me," said Albapot.

Raggy Christine and Albapot whizzed down together. Penguin went down sideways.

On the hall floor he found a stray sock. "Just what Owl needs for extra stuffing," said Penguin. "And to give him more Ooomph! This will be *my* birthday present."

And Penguin put the sock in his pocket.

"It must be about three weeks since Our Child went away," said Raggy Christine when at last they reached the kitchen.

"Don't be silly," said Albapot. "It's only lunch time."

"Are you *sure* they'll come back?" asked Raggy Christine.

"Sure as owls have hoots and penguins have flippers," said Albapot.

(Up in the attic Owl dreamed of more Time passing.)

Using her snappy legs Albapot climbed up on to the kitchen table. She found a scone on the bread board.

"This can be Owl's cake," said Albapot and she tucked it under her hat. Next to the scone was a jug of buttercups. Albapot pulled one out. "This is *my* present for Owl," she said.

At that moment a large black tiger rose from its basket. Penguin skidded under the table and quivered all over. Raggy Christine clung to one quivering flipper.

"It's only the cat," said Albapot loftily. "Just ignore him."

The tiger-cat considered Albapot with a canny eye, stalked to the door and eased himself through his flap. It snapped behind him like teeth.

"Are there any more?" asked Penguin weakly. "More cats, I mean."

"No," said Albapot, sliding down the table leg and bearing the buttercup like the lollipop lady her lollipop.

"Now," she said, "all we need is birthday hats."

"Lily has lots of bonnets," said Penguin.

"She looks so pretty in her bonnets," said Raggy Christine beginning to cry again. "Is it 'later' yet, Albapot?"

"Oh don't be so raggy-draggy!" said Albapot. "It's the middle of the afternoon and we've got to get back to Owl."

Climbing up the stairs took them a long time. Penguin was soon puffed out. Albapot and Raggy Christine had to push him up the second flight.

"Oh, hello!" said Owl when they reached the attic. "Is it my Very Old Birthday now? I've been having such fine dreams."

"It is," said Raggy Christine. "Happy Old Birthday, dear Owl," and she gave him the necklace.

"This is for extra Ooomph!" said Penguin, giving him the sock.

"And here's a piece of sunshine," said Albapot, giving him the buttercup.

Owl was quite overcome.

"Birthday hats," said Raggy Christine, waving Lily's bonnets.

It was growing dark when Albapot began slicing the birthday scone with a nail file. Just then they heard car doors slamming, a crunch of gravel, a high voice, a low voice, a coo and a gurgle and then the sound of a key in the front door.

With a single flap Penguin was up on the window sill.

"She's back!" he said. "Our Child's back!"

"Of course she's back," said Albapot. "What have I been telling you all day?"

"Now I can have a very happy old birthday," said Owl. "I think perhaps I might be twenty-one..."

There were footsteps on the stairs and Mrs Peppermint appeared with Lily in her arms.

Owl, Albapot, Penguin and Raggy Christine all shut their eyes.

"Well," said Mrs Peppermint, gazing at them, "I can't leave you four alone for a single minute, can I?"

Then she put Lily in her cot and sat all of them around her. Lily reached out her arms and laughed.